THE GREEN NINJA

ADAPTED BY TRACEY WEST

SCHOLASTIC INC.

ISBN 978-0-545-60798-8

12 11 10 9 8 7 6 5   14 15 16 17 18/0
Printed in the U.S.A.   40
First printing, August 2013

KID STUFF

"We've been training all day," Lloyd complained to his four ninja friends, Cole, Jay, Kai, and Zane.

"We have to get you ready to face your father," Cole reminded him. Lloyd was the Green Ninja — the only one who could take down the evil Lord Garmadon.

"But the latest edition of *Starfarer* just came in to Doomsday Comics," Lloyd said.

"Sorry, Lloyd," Kai said, "but as the Green Ninja, you don't have time for kid stuff."

Nya ran onto the deck of *Destiny's Bounty*, the ninja's flying ship. "Guys! Lord Garmadon has broken into the Ninjago Museum of Natural History."

"Let me guess," Lloyd said. "This mission is too dangerous for me, right?"

"Right!" the four ninja agreed.

    Inside the museum, Lord Garmadon held the Mega Weapon. It was a magical Weapon with the power to create.

    "Behold . . . the Grundle!" Lord Garmadon cried. He pointed to a skeleton of a huge, fierce-looking beast. "It is now extinct. But when it roamed Ninjago, it could track any ninja."

RISE OF THE GRUNDLE

Lord Garmadon pointed the Mega Weapon at the Grundle skeleton.

"Rise, Grundle!" he commanded.

The Weapon sizzled with blue sparks. Purple energy waves flowed over the skeleton.

The four ninja burst into the museum. Garmadon's Serpentine warriors tried to stop them.

But the ninja were fast. They jumped on top of the Grundle. The snake warriors charged them. They knocked Cole, Jay, and Zane off the Grundle's back.

Kai threw his sword at Lord Garmadon, knocking the Mega Weapon from his hand. The purple energy faded.

"Not again!" Lord Garmadon wailed.

"*Ha-ha!* We stopped him! It didn't work!" Jay cheered.

Lord Garmadon ran off. His snake warriors followed him, carrying a golden sarcophagus along with them.

"They're stealing it!" Kai cried. "After them!"

The ninja raced out of the museum and onto the street. The sarcophagus was heavy, so the snakes dropped it and escaped.

THE INCREDIBLE SHRINKING NINJA

"I don't remember that sarcophagus being so big," Kai remarked.

"Did it grow?" Jay asked.

"Or did we shrink?" wondered Zane.

Suddenly, Kai noticed their reflection in a store window. "Uh, guys?"

"We *shruuuunk*!" Jay screamed.

It was worse than that. The ninja had been turned back into kids!

"I hate being a kid!" Cole wailed. "You can't drive. Nobody listens to you. Oh, no . . . bedtimes!"

"Garmadon must have made us younger with the Mega Weapon," Zane guessed.

At that moment, a police car screeched to a stop next to them.

"Looks like we caught the museum thieves!" the police officer said.

The ninja tried to explain what had really happened, but the police didn't believe them. Cole, Jay, Kai, and Zane spent the night in the police station.

Back at the ship, Nya and Sensei Wu were worried about them.

"Lloyd, you're in charge of the *Bounty* while Nya and I have a look around town," Sensei Wu told him.

ONE ANCIENT MONSTER

The next morning, the police brought the ninja and the sarcophagus back to the museum.

"Thank you," said the director. "But what about the Grundle?" He pointed to an empty display case.

"You don't think it just walked out of here?" Jay wondered.

"It is possible that Garmadon made the Grundle younger, too," Zane said, "and brought it back to life!"

Jay ran up to the grownups. "You guys have to believe us! The Grundle has been brought back to life, and it's on the loose!"

The director and the police just laughed.

"You boys wait here until we call your parents to pick you up," an officer told them.

"We gotta get out of here — like, now!" Cole warned the other ninja.

The ninja pretended to be part of a school group. They sneaked out of the museum.

"This is so humiliating!" Jay wailed.

"We can't use Spinjitzu in these bodies," Zane pointed out. "We are no match for the Grundle."

"Then we have to get back to the *Bounty*!" Kai told his friends.

THE GRUNDLE RETURNS

Rawr! As the ninja hurried away, a loud roar came from the museum. A huge, red beast with sharp claws and teeth jumped off the roof.

It was the Grundle! The great beast hated the sunlight. It stomped off to find a place to sleep until the sun went down. The people of Ninjago screamed and ran when they saw it.

The ninja didn't see the Grundle. They found a pay phone and called the *Destiny's Bounty*.

Lloyd answered the phone. "Where are you?" he asked. "Sensei is out looking for you."

"We can't explain now," Jay said. "Just meet us at Buddy's Pizza in ten minutes — and bring our weapons."

Ten minutes later, Lloyd strolled into the pizza parlor.

"*Pssst!* Lloyd!" Kai whispered.

"Beat it, brat! I'm on a mission," Lloyd said. He thought Kai was just some kid.

"It's me, Kai!" Kai told him.

Lloyd gasped. "Whoa! What happened? You're . . . small!"

Cole, Jay, Kai, and Zane explained how Lord Garmadon had brought the Grundle to life — and turned them into kids at the same time.

"We can't defeat the Grundle until we're back to full strength," Kai said. "We need to find someone who knows how to fight that thing."

Lloyd grinned. "I think I know just the guy!"

COMIC-BOOK HEROES

Lloyd brought the ninja to a comics shop.

"We're not gonna pick up your stupid comic, Lloyd," Kai complained. "This is serious business!"

Suddenly, Jay let out a happy cry. "Look! A new issue of Daffy Dale!"

"Boys, this is Rufus McAllister, also known as Mother Doomsday," Lloyd said. "He owns this place."

"Rufus, what do you know about the Grundle?" Lloyd asked.

"I know all about that extinct beast," Rufus said. "One, its thick hide can't be hurt by any weapons. Two, it only hunts at night. And three, the only way to defeat it is with light."

The ninja nervously looked out the window. The sun was going down fast.

"The Illuma Sword is the best weapon for fighting a Grundle," Rufus said. "That is, if you can get close enough to use it."

"We'll take the light swords," Kai said eagerly.

"Not so fast," said Rufus. "You'll have to win these swords in a *Starfarer* trivia battle."

"Sign me up!" Lloyd said.

Before the contest started, Lloyd got a message to Sensei Wu.

"There is only one person who can turn the ninja back to normal," Sensei Wu told Nya. They hurried to Mystake's tea shop and explained their problem.

"You need Tomorrow's Tea," the old woman told them. "I should have one here somewhere."

Back at the comic shop, the contest began. Lloyd and two other kids answered questions about the *Starfarer* comic book and its hero, Fritz Donegan. It came down to Lloyd and just one other player.

"Lloyd! Lloyd! Lloyd!" the ninja cheered.

"Here's your final question," Rufus said. "In the latest issue, how does Fritz Donegan escape the Imperial Sludge?"

"B-b-but I didn't read the latest issue," Lloyd stammered.

Just then, the lights in the comic shop flickered. The whole room began to shake.

"It's here," Kai whispered.

ATTACK OF THE GRUNDLE

"What's here?" Rufus asked nervously.

They all looked up at the glass roof. A huge, scary figure loomed above them.

Crunch! A huge, scaly foot stomped down, smashing the glass.

Everyone screamed and ran.

Crash! The Grundle fell through the ceiling. The ninja quickly ran and pulled on ninja outfits on display in the store. They each grabbed an Illuma Sword and charged the Grundle.

Hii-yaah! One by one, they attacked the Grundle, but the monster swatted them away like flies.

The Grundle hovered over them, its huge jaw open. Green slime dripped from its mouth.

"Aaaaah!" the ninja screamed.

"I'll take care of this," Lloyd said. He created a ball of energy in his hands and hurled it at the Grundle.

Swat! The Grundle knocked down Lloyd with its tail.

Suddenly, Nya and Sensei Wu burst through the door.

Sensei Wu held up a jar of glowing liquid. "Use this! It will turn time forward. You will grow up and the Grundle will turn back into a pile of bones."

He tossed the jar to Jay.

"Wait!" Cole cried. "What will happen to Lloyd? He'll grow old, too."

"Just do it!" Lloyd cried.

"We can't take away your childhood," Jay said. "It's not fair."

The Grundle charged at the ninja, and they fell backward. The jar flew out of Jay's hands and landed in Lloyd's lap.

Lloyd stood up. He threw the jar at the Grundle. It hit him in the nose, and a purple mist floated out.

THE GREEN NINJA

Purple light swirled, and the Grundle whirled around as the magic tea took effect. Then the great beast quickly crumbled into a pile of bones.

When the dust cleared, Kai, Jay, Cole, and Zane stood up. They were taller — and older.

"We're not kids anymore," Cole realized.

Lloyd slowly got to his feet. He was taller. His hair was thicker. His voice was deeper.

"I'm . . . older," he said slowly.

"The time for the Green Ninja to face his destiny has grown nearer," said Sensei Wu.

Lloyd looked at his friends. "I'm ready," he said confidently.

Lloyd's mind was racing. Now that he was older, he would be able to control his Spinjitzu better. But did he really have what it took to become the legendary Green Ninja?

Sensei Wu seemed to read his mind. "The time until the final battle has become shorter," he said. "But the Green Ninja has grown stronger!"